The Wanderings of William Whiptail

VIVIAN HEAD
ILLUSTRATIONS BY BIDDY LEE

Published by PUIYIN W.L. PUBLISHING®

www.puiyinwlpublishing.com

www.puiyinwl.com

ISBN 978-0-9955398-6-0

Design by Vivian@Bookscribe
Illustrations by Biddy Lee

Printed and bound in Great Britain

Bid

William Whiptail wasn't going to waste a second ... no not a second. He knew instinctively when he saw the red pillar box outside his front door exactly what he had to do. He sat down at his tiny desk, fashioned out of an old children's pencil box, pulled a tiny stub of pencil out of the drawer and started to write in his very neatest handwriting.

Dear Cousin Peanut

I have lived in London for many a year now and have always yearned to travel and learn what life is like in the green, lush countryside. Food is plentiful here, but the hustle and bustle is taking its toll on my ageing bones and hence I am writing to you to let you know that I am on my way.

I have no idea of the trials and tribulations that are involved in travelling the numerous miles to your place of residence, so if I have not reached you in, say, a month's time, you'd better start worrying.

Yours affectionately

William Whiptail

There was much scurrying around putting the few meagre belongings he owned into two suitcases – a small green one and a larger one which was a sort of mustard yellow in colour. He made sure he had plenty of food, a map which would show him how to reach Trickle Wallop – a strange name he felt for anyone to live – and some warm clothes should the weather suddenly turn cold.

William left his little homestead underneath the floorboards of Number 10 Picksniff Road and scurried quickly across the pavement to avoid being trampled. He dragged his heavy suitcases behind him until he reached the base of the pillar box.

"Dilemma! I have a major dilemma," he said.

The problem was William was just too small to reach the slot in the pillar box to post his letter.

Disgruntled and more than a little upset he sat with his head in his hands. What was he to do?

Then it came to him as quick as a flash – he would use his suitcases as steps, climb on top and then he could post his letter. And this is exactly what he did. He didn't feel confident that the letter would actually reach his cousin as he had no stamps and the only address he could put on the envelope was: Cousin Peanut Pickory, Trickle Wallop, somewhere in the South East.

Mission accomplished, William climbed down from his cases, put on a brave face and started the journey through the crowded streets of London Town. Not an easy task for someone the size of a mouse.

"Well, scurry my whiskers!" he muttered as someone trod on the tip of his tail. No one noticed the little mouse, they were far too busy rushing around to get to the place they needed to be – wherever that place may be. William, on the other hand, knew exactly where he wanted to be and he just had to work out the best way of getting there.

The suitcases were definitely slowing him down and at this rate it would take him forever and a day to reach his destination. He decided the best option would be to perhaps only take the smaller of the cases, and keep his belongings to a bare minimum.

He found shelter at the back of an old paper stand and started to sift through the items in the larger suitcase, only taking the things he knew would definitely come in useful. As for the food – well he felt certain he would meet some kind samaritans on the way who would be only too willing to give him a crust of bread and a morsel of cheese.

He now had a new dilemma – what to do with his large suitcase and the remainder of his belongings. He knew there were many homeless mice and rats living in the gutters of London who would be only too pleased to help themselves. He didn't have to walk far until he came across what looked like a pile of old newspapers. As he got closer he could see the paper rise and fall with the breathing of whatever was beneath them and the occasional snore which definitely gave the occupant away.

"Ahem, excuse me," William said quite loudly.

There was no response from the pile of newspaper and so he coughed loudly and pushed the pile gently with his foot. A little whiskered nose poked out from underneath and as the rest of his face appeared William could see he was more than a little disgruntled.

"What yer want?" said the little mouse.

"Well, if you're going to be like that, I'll give my case to someone else."

"Case, what case?" the mouse said twitching his nose from side to side.

"This case," said William pointing to the larger of the two at his feet. "I am going travelling and it is too big for me to carry, but it would make an excellent bed and there are also some clothes and food in there if it would be of any use to you."

The little mouse's attitude immediately softened to one of gratitude.

"Wow," he said, "no one, and I say no one, 'as ever been nice to me before."

"Well, I am, and I hope you find it very cosy."

His task completed, William put on one of his many scarves, took the much lighter suitcase in his hand and continued his journey glad that he had been able to help a fellow mouse in need.

He stopped quite a few times to nibble on some nice Cheddar the kind people at Number 10 had accidentally dropped on the floor. His feet were starting to ache and his fur was clinging to his body because the day was getting warmer and warmer. The air was stifling in the city, walking between the tall buildings and dodging all sorts of obstacles.

He eventually reached Putney Green and noticed to his delight a bright yellow and red circus tent pitched right in the centre. Ooh, he loved the circus. So William headed towards the tent to see if he could get in to see one of the shows.

He was about to duck underneath the canvas to get inside the tent when a hand grabbed the back of his neck.

"Oi, mate, where do you think you're going?"

"I... I... I... just w-w-wanted to s-s-see the circus," William stuttered.

After all the voice did sound rather gruff.

"OK, mate, where's yer ticket then?"

William stood tall and dared to turn round to see who was confronting him. He nearly burst out laughing when he saw the gruff voice was coming from a mouse dressed in a stripy clown's outfit with a bright red nose and a pointy hat with a bobble on the top.

William guffawed out loud but stopped abruptly when the clown said,

"Who do yer think you're sniggering at?"

"Well, you're a clown, aren't people meant to laugh at clowns?" William replied.

"Er, yes, but only when I'm being funny!"

"Sorry, but clowns always make me laugh. Won't you let me in to see the show I'll give you a bit of my extra special cheese."

At the mention of cheese the clown wiggled his bright, oversized, red nose and sniffed the air.

"Cheese, you say. Now a mouse could be tempted by a bit of cheese wouldn't you say."

William opened his little green suitcase and rummaged around inside until he found the piece of paper containing his last few remaining pieces of cheese and offered one to the clown.

The clown took it greedily and then held up the corner of the canvas to allow William to enter.

"Remember to laugh extra loud when Baggy Britches – that's me by the way – comes in carrying a load of balloons and a little bluebird pops them all."

"Oh, I most certainly will. And thank you."

The tent was already full to the brim with mice of all ages and a few rather unsavoury looking rats who seemed to have taken over the front seats.

William took a seat at the back. They were tiered so it meant he had a good view of the arena so long as he kept his glasses on. He really couldn't see very well without his glasses these days.

Oh how William enjoyed the circus, with the ringmaster prancing

Bid

around in his tall black hat and cane announcing the next act. There were mice walking on a tightrope, then others swinging about on the trapeze sometimes daring to hang by just their tail. Then came two mice on unicycles who rode round and round the ring while the crowd sang along to 'Three Blind Mice' followed by a juggler.

He didn't have to remember to laugh at the clown because he was indeed extremely funny, especially when four little bluebirds flew into the ring and popped each one of his colourful balloons.

The main act of the day was Chickita the ballerina chicken in her bright pink tutu and three-toed ballet shoes. She danced to the music of Swan Lake – which William thought a little strange as the music was about swans – but Chickita was so graceful he really didn't mind. She twirled and jumped in the air, her wings flapping and her legs going in all directions. She really was a joy to watch and William clapped loudly when her dance came to an end. He really was having such fun.

However, the act William loved the best were two little mice who danced around a large bowl of strawberries to the tune of 'Strawberry Fields Forever'. William clapped and cheered so loudly that the two mice asked if he would like to join them. He didn't need asking twice, he ran down to the circus ring, jumped up onto the side of the glass bowl and danced and danced until his little legs ached. Afterwards they went round the audience and handed each one a bright red strawberry to eat. It was great to see all the young mice with strawberry juice all round their whiskers.

William decided it had been the perfect start to his adventures.

By the time the circus was over the sun had gone down and it was starting to get dark. William had no idea where he was going to sleep, he really hadn't thought that far ahead, but once again his friend the clown came to his rescue.

"Enjoyed the show did yer?" he asked.

"Absolutely spiffing," replied William.

"Then why the long face?"

"I haven't been very clever in planning my journey to Trickle Wallop and so I have no idea where I am going to sleep tonight," William said a little glumly.

"Well... I might be able to 'elp you there," the clown said, "if you don't mind bunking down with one of the unicyclists."

"Not at all, old chap, not at all."

The clown led William round the back of the tent to a tiny caravan and knocked on the door.

They waited a while but no one seemed to be there. Suddenly William heard a little squeaky voice directly behind them. They both turned round and William recognised the mouse as one of the unicyclists that had performed earlier.

"What you want Baggy Britches?" the young mouse asked.

"Don't suppose you'd be prepared to share your bed for the night for a bit of cheese, would yer?"

Sprinkle, for that was the mouse's name, wiggled his tiny nose, furrowed his brow for a second, then nodded in agreement. William only had one small piece of Cheddar left in his small green suitcase, but if it meant he had a bed for the night it would be worth giving it up.

The caravan was quite cramped due to a large metal Oxo tin at one end which William could see served as a bed.

"Hope it's good enough for yer?" Sprinkle said. "Now where's that cheese I'm starving?"

William rummaged around in his suitcase, unwrapping his last piece of cheese and handing it over to Sprinkle a little reluctantly. Then he took out his blue striped nightshirt and matching nightcap and got himself ready for bed. He really was extremely tired and the bed really did look rather inviting.

They both climbed into the Oxo tin and although William was a little too long he managed to lie down even though his feet and tail were sticking out the end. Sprinkle told him that he was only sixteen and had always lived with

OXO
48 ORIGINAL CUBES
Bid

the circus people because his father was the other unicyclist and his mother worked on the trapeze. He said he loved the life because they got to see so many different places.

William was fascinated but couldn't stop himself from yawning. He was quite relieved when Sprinkle actually talked himself to sleep and William could close his eyes and drift off into the land of dreams. Just before he fell asleep he wondered what tomorrow would bring.

The following morning the sun had forgotten to get up and the clouds were shedding their tears. William looked out of the caravan's windows and wished he had packed a raincoat. He really hadn't thought this through at all.

"What's up mate?" Sprinkle said climbing lazily out of his makeshift bed.

"Well... you see I'm trying to get to Trickle Wallop to go and live with my cousin Peanut, but I really haven't thought it through. I know it's somewhere in the South East but how on earth I am going to get there? And it's raining!" he said rather sulkily.

"Come on William, you'll feel a whole lot better after some breakfast. And I think I might know somebody who can help you."

William was intrigued but decided not to ask any more questions for the moment because his stomach really was grumbling rather loudly.

Sprinkle handed William a large piece of plastic bag to put over his head and told him to follow him outside. They ran trying to avoid the larger drops of rain to a bigger caravan on the other side of the circus tent.

As they reached the caravan the door opened and Sprinkle was enveloped in a great big hug. With his face still pressed into her chest he mumbled,

"This is my mum, William."

"Welcome, William. I hope you enjoyed the show last night and I have to say you danced really well round the strawberry bowl, perhaps you'd like a job," she said with a big smile on her face.

"Oh... er... um..." William didn't know quite what to say, he suddenly felt rather cumbersome and embarrassed in front of the rather slim trapeze artist.

"What I think William would like is some grub," said Sprinkle having managed to wriggle himself out of his mother's clutches, "his tummy has been making some dreadful noises! I really don't think we should keep him waiting any longer."

They all laughed and William forgot to be embarrassed as he sat down to a rare feast of crumpets covered with delicious butter, roasted chesnuts, and his very favourite homemade cheese straws.

After breakfast they sat down on one of the beanbags in the corner of the caravan and William dared to ask what Sprinkle had been talking about earlier.

"You said you might know someone who could help me?" he asked tentatively.

"Yes I do. They are called the 'Wise Ones' because they are wise I guess. My Uncle Runcible told me about how they had helped him when his circus tent was burnt down and he didn't have enough money to buy a new one."

William was intrigued.

"How would I find these 'Wise Ones'?" he asked.

"Once you have crossed the Common you will come to an area of woodland. You will see a path that goes through the centre of the trees and, although it twists and turns a lot, it will eventually lead you to a clearing where there are two large trees. If the 'Wise Ones' are at home there will be two red-topped toadstools in the clearing. All you have to do is rub the top of the right-hand toadstool three times in a circular motion and the 'Wise Ones' will come out from their underground dwelling and you can speak with them."

"Thank you so much Sprinkle for helping me and letting me sleep in your bed," William said shaking Sprinkle's little paw.

"Oi mate, don't shake me 'and off," he said in his broad London accent.

"And thank you Mrs Sprinkle for such a wonderful breakfast, I am indebted to you."

Mrs Sprinkle smiled and told William he was welcome any time.

It was still raining as they made their way back to the smaller caravan to pick up his little green case. Once inside Sprinkle showed William how to make the piece of plastic bag into a cape with a hood by using tiny little safety pins. He was sad to say goodbye to his new friend, but William was eager to continue his journey to Trickle Wallop.

It seemed a long way across the Common before he reached the start of the wood. The rain was quite heavy and the wind kept blowing the plastic hood off his head. William was starting to feel a little miserable and wondered whether he should turn back for home. Eventually a gust of wind blew his makeshift cape off his back and up into the branches of a tree.

William huddled beneath the canopy of a large toadstool to shelter from the rain. His fur was soaking wet, his glasses were steamed up and he felt thoroughly miserable as he looked down at his little toes which were all wrinkled from the rain. He kept going over the words little Sprinkle had told him about the 'Wise Ones' but wondered whether they were just a figment of the young mouse's imagination.

He stayed under the shelter of the toadstool for what seemed liked hours but eventually the sun woke up. William peered out from beneath the toadstool and noticed to his delight there was indeed a windy path that led through the middle of the trees. It was a little muddy and he had to be careful not to trip over the slippery tree roots that were hidden by the fallen leaves. He trod carefully winding this way and that until he came to a clearing exactly as Sprinkle had described it. Right in the middle of the clearing were two large trees and to his delight he noticed two large red-topped toadstools sitting beneath them.

He crossed the clearing looking all around him to see if anyone was around. When he reached the toadstools he reached up to touch the one on the right-hand side and made three small circles with his paw.

Nothing happened for a second or two and William wondered whether Sprinkle had been leading him a merry dance, when all of a sudden there was a bright flash of orange light and a door opened in the base of one of the trees. William's eyes came out on stalks, he was so taken aback with surprise.

He watched as three mice, all wearing golden crowns, stepped out from

beneath the roots and went to sit on a mossy patch between the two large trees. They said nothing but as they looked at William the sky went dark and one single bright star shone down lighting up their faces. William was too shocked to say a word.

"William Whiptail, how may we help you?" the middle mouse asked.

"How... how... how do you know my name?" William stuttered.

"We know everything," they all said together.

"Then you know I am trying to get to Trickle Wallop?" he said swallowing hard. It all seemed so surreal and he had to pinch himself to see if he was dreaming. The pinch hurt so he knew he definitely wasn't dreaming and the three mice were real.

"Yes, indeed."

William's legs were shaking so much he wasn't sure how much longer they would hold him up, so he sat down on a mound of damp leaves with his little green suitcase tucked under his arm.

"What have you got there?" the wise mouse on the right asked.

"My... my... suitcase," William said, a little uncertain what their intentions were. He really didn't want to lose the last of his belongings.

"Is it a magic suitcase?" the wise mouse on the left asked.

"No, no, I don't think so," William replied.

"Are you sure? Have you tried rubbing it?" the same mouse said.

"R...r...rubbing it?" William queried.

"Yes, that's what I said, rubbing it. Try rubbing the top of the case with your right paw in a circular motion while saying the words 'Rumtirarra-grant-me-a-wish'. But think very carefully before making that wish because you will only have three and then the magic will run out."

"In that case 'Wise Ones'," William said, "I think I will keep my wishes until I know exactly what I need."

The three 'Wise Ones' looked at each other and nodded. "Very wise indeed William, perhaps you are not so stupid after all."

William felt a little insulted at the use of the word stupid, but if what they were saying was really true then he didn't want to do anything to upset the three mice. For the moment he had to take their word for it that he really did have a magic suitcase and he guessed he would find out in good time.

"Thank you for your advice," William said politely. "I think I will be on my way now."

He bowed, as he felt that was rather appropriate because they were wearing crowns, then walked backwards so that he didn't have to show his back to the three mice out of respect.

By the time he reached the other side of the clearing the sky was blue again and the three wise mice were nowhere to be seen. He hoped he would remember the magic words and wondered whether he should write them down. Then he realised he had neither paper nor pencil so instead he kept repeating the words over and over again in his head.

He walked a little further until he came to a river and sat down on the bank because his furry little legs would carry him no further. He took out the packed lunch Mrs Sprinkle had made for him, spread down an old piece of newspaper to sit on and then tucked in. He really was very hungry and very tired. He knew it was getting late in the day because the sun was dropping lower and lower in the sky and he now had the problem again of where to sleep the night. He also had the worry of thinking about his three wishes. He didn't want to waste them, he knew they would be vital to him reaching his destination.

He would have liked to have rubbed the case and asked for a nice warm bed for the night, but he knew that would be a wasted wish and wouldn't help him on his journey to Trickle Wallop. He was about to lay down on his piece of newspaper when a little head appeared between the bullrushes. At first it made William jump, but when he realised it was only a water rat he smiled. He had two long teeth that stuck out in the front and his fur was sleek and dark from being in the water.

"Hello," William said.

"Hello back," the water rat said staring at William.

"I don't suppose you know a dry place I could sleep for the night do you?" William asked, not really expecting a positive reply.

"If you don't mind sharing with my family, I have a very comfortable home in the bank. Mind you, you'll have to crawl about a metre to reach the bed chamber."

"That's very kind of you and I am sure I can manage the tunnel," William said getting to his feet.

The water rat, whose name was Mangus William discovered, scrambled up the slippery riverbank with ease. William, on the other hand, struggled to get a grip due to the fact that he was trying to keep his precious case dry. Although he didn't know whether it was really magic or not he didn't want to risk losing it in the murky river water.

Mangus reached down and took his paw and helped to pull William up to the entrance of his home. The door had been made out of mud and helped to keep out intruders. It was very dark inside but as they got further and further into the underground tunnel, William could hear a lot of chattering and laughter.

He was out of breath by the time they reached the bed chamber. Sitting round a little table made out of the heads of bullrushes sat five little water rats and Mrs Mangus.

"Welcome," she said with a broad smile on her face. "Won't you join us for supper?"

The smell of fish and crustaceans turned William's stomach but he really didn't want to seem ungrateful.

"Thank you," he replied. "I would love to only I've just eaten my supper up on the bank."

"That's a shame we've got some lovely little minnows, a couple of frog's legs and a couple of crunchy spiders. You're missing a treat."

It took all of William's willpower not to heave at the thought of eating a spider or even a frog's leg and he was so thankful to Mrs Sprinkle for her parcel of food. He hadn't eaten every morsel, he had saved some for his breakfast. He heaved a sigh of relief and sat down with the family while they ate their supper.

"I will sleep with the children," Mrs Mangus said, "if you don't mind sharing with my husband."

"It would be a real pleasure."

For the second time on his journey William changed into his stripy nightshirt and nightcap and this time settled himself down next to Mangus on a bed of reeds. It wasn't nearly as comfortable as the Oxo tin but it was dry and warm and, once William had got used to the smell of Mangus' fishy breath, he managed to fall asleep without too much trouble. His dreams that night were of the circus and the fun he had had with Sprinkle.

William had a dream he was flying through the air and he could feel the breeze trying to lift his nightcap off his head.

He lifted his paw to stop his cap from blowing off and then something made him open his eyes. He hadn't been dreaming, he really was up in the air and a huge pair of eyes were staring down at him.

"Look Molly, I've found a mouse and he's wearing a nightshirt," said the little boy.

"Don't be silly Tom, mice don't wear clothes!"

"I'm telling you he's wearing a nightshirt and a matching cap. Come see."

The little girl came over and peered into Tom's hand. William didn't dare move, in fact he didn't think he could move he was frozen in fear.

"Oh, you're right," Molly said. "Where did you find him?"

"Right here on the bank. He was asleep."

"What are you going to do with him?" Molly asked.

"I'm going to keep him as a pet, he's so cute."

William felt himself being pushed into a coat pocket and everything went dark. This was a disaster, a disaster of the most mammoth kind. If he ever needed a wish it was right now, but he would need his little green suitcase if he wanted to make magic.

He could feel tears welling up in his eyes, but suddenly remembered he had tucked his suitcase under his nightshirt for safe keeping before he went to sleep last night. He fumbled around in the dark and sure enough he felt the comforting lump of his case nestled against his belly. He immediately felt better but wondered how on earth he had ended up outside on the bank when he had gone to sleep in the water rats' home.

What he didn't know was that he had snored so loudly in the night it had kept the whole water rat family awake. Mr and Mrs Mungus had quite literally pushed William along the tunnel, lifted him down the bank and left him to sleep beside the reeds on the riverbank.

William bumped against the boy's hip as he started to walk away from the river. He managed to pull the suitcase from under his nightshirt and rubbed the surface in a circular motion, but then he stopped. The fright of being held by a human had made him forget the magic words and he panicked. He tried what he believed were the right words but nothing happened and his tummy started to ache as he became more and more frightened.

Calm down, William, he told himself. Calm down. This will never do.

He took several deep breaths until his heart stopped racing and then rubbed the case again, this time chanting 'Rumtirarra-grant-me-a-wish' three times as he had been instructed.

Immediately the pocket filled with a bright blueish light and there was a loud popping sound like bubbles bursting.

William didn't know how long he had to make his wish so he said very quickly, "I would like a boat and a paddle to take me down the river."

Within seconds William could feel himself spinning round and round in a tunnel of swirling mist. It made him feel a little sick and he wished it would stop. He was just about to scream when everything became calm and he found himself sitting in a little blue rowing boat with a paddle in one hand.

He was no longer wearing his nightgown and nightcap and his glasses were now in place on his nose. He panicked in case he had lost his little green suitcase, but he needn't have worried it was right there in front of his nose. The three 'Wise Ones' had told the truth, he really did have a magic suitcase. William smiled.

He stopped for a while by the side of the river to eat the rest of Mrs Sprinkles' food parcel and then started on the next part of his journey to Trickle Wallop.

After looking at the map to see in which direction he needed to go, William grasped the paddle in both hands and started to push the little boat through the water. His long tail kept getting caught round the paddles at first, so he had to make sure he kept it in the boat. The weather was a little cloudy but warm and William could feel himself start to relax and enjoy his journey as he passed down the tranquil river away from London Town.

Several animals waved to him as he allowed the current to carry him downriver. There was a beaver busy gnawing away at an old treetrunk, several squirrels and another family of water rats and William wondered if they were relatives of Mungus. He was still curious as to how he came to be on the riverbank that morning instead of in bed with Mungus, but he guessed he would never know. Next he passed a heron who had a fish in his mouth. He couldn't speak but he did wave one of his extremely long legs as William passed by.

William wasn't used to so much exercise and after a couple of hours of paddling he started to feel really sleepy. He put the paddle in the bottom of the boat and then lay down and closed his eyes, allowing the current to carry him along. He must have drifted off to sleep because he was suddenly woken by a gentle bump as the boat hit the riverbank and became entangled in some reeds.

What he didn't realise was that a rather large water snake was curled up asleep in the reeds and he wasn't at all happy about being woken up.

William sat up and rubbed his eyes to try and wake himself up unaware that the snake was glaring at him from behind a rather large bulrush. It uncurled its body and started slithering silently towards the boat. William, who had his back to the bank, was totally unaware that he was being watched. Suddenly he felt the little boat rock and he had to hold onto the sides to avoid being tipped out into the water. Gradually the rocking became more and more violent and the boat was starting to fill with water.

He turned round to see who was rocking the boat but was struck dumb at the sight of an enormous serpent's head peering over the side of the boat and its eyes swirling round and round in circles. Then William saw its forked tongue flick out of its huge mouth and before he knew it he was lifted up and was staring down into the darkness of the snake's throat. He knew it was useless to struggle because the snake would only tighten its grip. He had no idea what to do because his little magic suitcase was still in the boat. He was about to panic as he started to slide further into the snake's mouth when he remembered he had some acorns in his pocket for emergencies and this was definitely an emergency. Luckily his arms were pinned to his sides and he managed to move one enough to get his hand into his pocket. He took out a handful of acorns and starting throwing them down the snake's throat. Nothing happened for a few seconds, but after the third and then the fourth acorn the snake got such violent hiccoughs that he opened his mouth wide and William plopped out and into the water beside the boat.

Making sure the snake was distracted he clambered over the far side of the boat, grabbed the paddle and pushed away from the bank with all his might, his heart still thumping in his chest. That was one adventure he really would rather not have had and he hoped the rest of his day would be a lot better. He felt and looked like a drowned rat, even though he was a mouse. He paddled further down the river to make sure the snake didn't follow him and then when he thought it was safe to stop, he dropped his homemade anchor – a large stone on the end of a piece of string – and got his old tin mug out of his suitcase and started to bail out the water from the bottom of the boat. When he was happy the worst of the water was out he looked at the map to see where he was.

As he studied the map William realised he wouldn't be able to go much further by river as it would take him in the wrong direction. He was quite sad at the thought of leaving his little boat behind and looked around to see if there was anyone around.

Apart from some birds singing, the rustle of the reeds in the breeze and the lapping of the water on the side of the boat, there was no sound.

Then William heard a very loud and deep croak and a splash which seemed to come from underneath the boat. He nearly panicked again, fearing the snake had followed him downriver.

"Oi, you nearly gave me a headache with that rock you dropped!"

A rather large, knobbly looking toad popped his head out of the water. His eyes looked a little bit angry and when he gripped the side of the boat with his webbed front feet William wondered if he was about to be tipped into the water again.

"I'm really sorry, I didn't know there was anyone under the boat you see," William explained.

"No excuse, no excuse, people have to live here you know!"

"I... I... I don't suppose you'd have any use for a boat, would you?" William asked trying to calm the toad down.

The toad made a funny noise and distended his throat before swimming all around the boat and checking it for any holes.

"Why, you selling?" he asked, not quite so grumpily.

"No, I'm not selling, but I would like to give it to someone who could make use of it because I no longer need it you see."

"Well..." and the toad paused, "I don't have much use for a boat because I swim everywhere but I do know a family of rats who live further up the bank who would make good use of it."

"Splendid, superb," William said clapping his hands. "Point me in the right direction and I will go there immediately.

"Follow me," the toad said and swam off down the river.

William immediately grabbed the paddle and pushed himself away from the riverbank. It was hard to keep up with the toad, but luckily he kept stopping and putting his head above water to make sure the little blue boat was following him.

After about fifteen minutes they came to a narrow point in the river where there was a little inlet surrounded by beautiful dog roses that blushed in the afternoon sun. William steered the boat into the inlet, climbed carefully onto the bank and tied the end of the boat to a nearby tree trunk with the piece of string that was attached to the front.

The toad sat in the water and blinked his enormous eyes to clear them of water. "If you walk over there you will come to a little green door at the base of a large oak tree. Knock on the door and Bingo will answer. They're a friendly bunch of rats so no need to be nervous."

William wanted to say thank you but by the time he had turned back to look at the toad he had submerged under the water and, apart from a few bubbles on the surface, he was nowhere to be seen.

Remembering to pick up his magic green suitcase, William walked off in the direction of the large oak which he could see in the distance. He knocked quite hard on the door to make sure someone heard him. He could hear quite a lot of scurrying noises before it was finally opened to reveal a rather scruffy looking rat who looked as though he had just got out of bed.

"Er... em... the toad that lives in the river sent me to see you," William said feeling a little bit put off by the rat's appearance. He was used to seeing rats like him living in the sewers of London but he hadn't expected to see one looking quite so rough out in the countryside. It really was quite offputting.

"And?" the rat said raising his voice as he finished the word. William could see that he was being a nuisance and decided he would leave.

"Oh, nothing. Sorry to have bothered you."

"It can't have been nothing otherwise Toady wouldn't have sent you. Sorry I didn't mean to sound grumpy I guess I got out of the wrong side of bed this morning," the rat said apologetically. "My name's Nimbus," and he held out his sweaty little paw in greeting.

William shook his paw and started to explain that he had a boat that he no longer needed and wondered whether the rat would be interested.

"Interested? I am more than interested," he said enthusiastically. "My gang will be so excited because none of us like swimming and we absolutely hate getting our coats wet."

"Gang?" William queried.

"Yes, you see we left London two years ago and started up this sort of commune. It's great, although it's much harder to find food down here."

William nodded.

"Well, where's this boat then?" Nimbus asked.

"Ah, yes, the boat. Follow me down to the river and I will show you."

Nimbus closed the door and followed William to the riverbank. He was delighted when he saw the little blue boat in such good condition, but then his smile changed to a frown. "Ah, you see we have no money and..."

William didn't give him time to finish his sentence.

"No need for the glum face, young man, I don't want your money. I just want the boat to go to a good home because I no longer need it."

Nimbus was gobsmacked. A FREE boat. This mouse must be mad.

"The only thing I would like is some food if you have any to spare," William said now feeling a lot more confident.

"Food! Food! You can have as much food as you like from our larder. We went on a raiding spree in the local village last night so there should be plenty to suit you," Nimbus said cheerfully. "A FREE boat!!" he repeated and kept repeating it all the way back to his home.

William left the den under the tree with a parcel of food that he knew would last him at least three days and he went on his way a very happy mouse.

He first looked at his map which showed he was about half way towards his destination of Trickle Wallop. He needed to follow Pigtrotter Lane until he came to the village of Gallumpton and then follow the railway track which should take him to within five miles of Trickle Wallop. Thanks to his magic suitcase and the first wish, he had taken quite a lot of travelling time off his journey.

He found Pigtrotter Lane quite easily on the other side of the village and starting walking along quite merrily eating wild strawberries out of the hedgerows. They were so sweet he found he wanted more and more.

He was just reaching over to pick a nice plump juicy one when a mouse on a bike rushed past at a great speed knocking William forwards into the hedgerow. His face squashed into the juicy strawberry he was about to pick

and red juice ran down his face. He felt quite cross because the mouse didn't bother to stop and in fact she was going so fast her hat blew off and her basket, which was full of flowers, was getting emptier by the minute as she bumped along the stony lane.

"Hey!" William shouted after her. "Manners!"

But the little mouse didn't turn around which made William even more angry. He quickly rubbed his suitcase without thinking that he might be wasting a wish and chanted 'Rumtirarra-grant-me-a-wish' three times. There was a bright flash of blue light, the sound of bubbles popping and William quickly made his wish. "I wish that rude little mouse would fall off her bike and that it belonged to me!"

He knew it wasn't a very kind wish and that he shouldn't ask for such a thing, but he hated people with bad manners. No sooner had he said the words than he heard a clatter and a scream as the little mouse toppled over onto the grass verge. Luckily she didn't seem to be hurt because she stood up, brushed herself off and was about to jump back on her bike when William held out his hand and the little mouse seemed to freeze on the spot. By the time William reached her he watched as she simply vanished into thin air in a puff of blue smoke. It was a shame really because she really was a pretty little mouse, but it did leave William the bike which was lying by the side of the road. He really was starting to enjoy his new magic powers.

He put his little green suitcase into the basket amongst the remaining flowers, climbed onto the saddle and started to pedal down the lane. He was a little bit wobbly at first because he hadn't ridden a bicycle since he was a child, but he soon got the hang of it. He bumped away over the pebbles, being careful to avoid the potholes, and started whistling to himself. He really was enjoying his journey so far, apart from the incident with the snake.

He had been cycling for about half an hour when he found his way blocked by a large farm gate which was secured with an enormous padlock. William really didn't want to have to turn around and go all the way back so he looked at the map to see if there was another way. To his dismay he found the only path through to the village of Gallumpton was via Black Chook Farm. All he needed to do now was find the person who owned the key and get the gate unlocked. He knew he could just climb through the bars of the gate, that was not a problem, but that meant he would have to leave his bicycle behind and he really had become very fond of it.

He propped the bike up against the gate post, climbed through the lower bars of the gate and started walking down the farm track towards a rather ramshackle barn. He had probably only taken about a dozen steps when he heard a very loud squawking and was confronted by an enormous black cockerel flapping his wings and who obviously had attitude.

William stopped, he was far too small to mess with something that big and strong and he certainly couldn't afford to use his last wish because he didn't know when he might need it. He decided to stand his ground and spoke to the cockerel to see if he would see reason.

"Excuse me, sir," hoping the title 'sir' might soften him a little. "Is there any way you could unlock the gate so I might cycle through the farm?"

The cockerel puts its wings on its hips, stood as tall as he could, and said "Cock-a-doodle-do, now here's a to-do, you want to get through, and I don't know what to do."

"Do you always speak in rhyme?" William asked politely.

To which the cockerel replied, "Cock-a-doodle-do, that's how I'll speak to you, now what do you want me to do?"

"I'd like you to open the gate, mate, so I can get on my bike and hike!" William wasn't very good at this rhyming lark but he thought it was appropriate to respond in a similar way.

"Cock-a-doodle-do, now here's what I'll do. But I warn you it won't be

Bid.

fun, because the farmer's got a gun, and he'll shoot a rat like you!"

William was not happy at being called a rat and he stood up as tall as his little legs would allow but he still only came up to the cockerel's knees.

"Now look here, I'm not a rat!" he said, completely forgetting to speak in rhyme.

"If you're not a rat, then drat, I suppose you're a mouse that lives in a house."

It was really hard work talking to a creature that only communicated in rhyme and William was starting to lose his temper.

"Cock-a-doodle-do, are you going to let me through, or are you going to keep up this game which I might add is rather lame!"

The cockerel looked a bit sullen when William spoke to him in such a manner and he thought he could see a small tear in the corner of his beady eye. "I'm sorry," the cockerel said in a completely different tone of voice. "You see we have had problems with rats stealing eggs from my wives and the farmer has told me he will cook me at Christmas if I don't keep them away from the farm."

William suddenly felt rather sorry for the cockerel who all of a sudden came up with a really good idea. "Why don't you just slide your bike underneath the gate, it's only small, and then I won't have to go and get the farmer and neither of us will get into trouble."

"Smart thinking," said William. "Why on earth didn't I think of that!"

He walked back to the gate with the large cockerel strutting behind him. He climbed back through the first set of bars and then lay his bike down on its side and pushed it underneath the gate just as the chook had suggested. The handlebars got stuck at one point, but the cockerel bent down and used all his strength to pull it through. He wasn't such an angry chook after all.

William thanked him again, got on his bicycle and merrily cycled off through the farmyard keeping a keen eye out for anyone with a gun.

He reached the village of Gallumpton before nightfall and found a very cosy disused coal bunker to make a bed for the night. He collected a load of dry grass from the owner's rather overgrown garden, lay it on the base of the bunker and then laid his sheet of newspaper carefully over the top.

He had some supper from the supplies the rats had given him, changed into his stripy nightshirt and nightcap and lay down on his makeshift bed. He was asleep within minutes.

The following morning William woke to the sound of the cockerel crowing to welcome the new day. William smiled, he wasn't nearly as proud and grumpy as he had first appeared. He was just scared that the farmer would turn him into a nice meal and so was making extra sure there were no intruders.

After breakfast, William decided to have a walk round the village before setting off again on his bike. He really was rather enjoying the peace and quiet of the countryside, even though it was very different to life in the city.

The sun was up early and it was already very hot by the time William reached the little village green. It was only a tiny hamlet with about a dozen houses, a public house called 'The Proud Chook' – he knew where they got that name from – and a village shop which incorporated a Post Office. There weren't many humans about which was nice, but he did see two mice

sheltering under a toadstool and decided he would like to speak with them.

He walked across the village green in the direction of the toadstool and as he approached he introduced himself. "Hello, I'm William and I'm on my way to visit my cousin in Trickle Wallop."

"Hello," said the older mouse. "My name is Casper and this is my son Cornelius. We are waiting for the mouse bus to take my son to school."

Cornelius just waved his little paw and William waved back and smiled.

"Do you know Trickle Wallop?" William asked. "Do you think it will take me long to get there?"

"If you are walking then about two days by a mouse's whisker," Casper replied.

"Well, I do have a bike, so perhaps I can make it there a little bit quicker," he said hopefully.

"Perhaps," Casper said.

William was so busy chatting that he hadn't noticed another mouse join the queue for the bus. He turned and smiled and what he saw quite literally took his breath away. She was the prettiest little mouse he had ever seen, with her two cute ears poking out from a red spotted mop cap. William had never had a real girlfriend, he had never had the confidence to ask anyone out, and he could feel his heart beating very fast. In fact it was beating so

loud he was certain the other mice would be able to hear it. His little paws started to sweat but he knew he couldn't let this opportunity go by without introducing himself.

"Hello," he said very quietly, "my name is William."

The little mouse looked extremely nervous and her nose twitched rather rapidly and her eyes opened wide.

"Please don't be frightened," said William. "I'm just a traveller on my way to see my cousin Peanut who lives in Trickle Wallop."

The little mouse didn't say anything for ages, she just stared at him with her big, beautiful, brown eyes. Eventually she stood up on her hind legs and said in the softest voice, "Hello, my name's Minka."

William was almost breathless at the sound of her voice and he couldn't stop staring at her even though he knew it was rude.

"Do you live in the village?" he dared to ask.

She looked towards the ground feeling a little intimidated by William's stare. "Yes," she said eventually. "I live over the Post Office with my cousin and her son called Marmalade. It's a strange name isn't it but you see he fell in a bowl of marmalade when he was really tiny and the name just stuck."

William laughed. "I think that's a great name and I particularly liked the pun." He wasn't sure whether she had intended it to be funny but it had made William chuckle.

He was about to ask her another question when the community bus turned up and they all had to say their goodbyes. William waved to all three of them until the bus was out of sight and then returned to his coal bunker to pick up his little green suitcase and his bike.

He looked at his map one more time to make sure he was taking the right road, climbed onto the saddle of his bike and off he went in search of Trickle Wallop. He wondered how many more adventures he would have before he arrived at his destination.

As he cycled along in the sunshine all he could think about was Minka and how stunningly beautiful she was. He had never felt this way before about a girl mouse and he wondered whether this was what love felt like. He had little butterflies doing somersaults in his tummy, his paws were clammy and his heart wouldn't stop racing. He really did feel rather strange.

For now his mission was to find Peanut and settle into his new home, but he had a feeling that wouldn't be the last time he would see Minka. Or at least he hoped it wouldn't.

He cycled as fast as his little legs would carry him until his tummy told him it was lunchtime due to its very loud grumbling noises.

He stopped by the side of a pond on a grassy bank where loads of wild buttercups, dandelions and tiny violets were growing in abundance. He laid down his piece of newspaper and what food he had left. After he had eaten he lay back and let the sun warm his face. He hadn't felt so peaceful and happy in years, he had definitely done the right thing leaving the city.

He closed his eyes and thought of Minka and then he felt something soft touch the end of his nose. He opened his eyes to find a squirrel staring down at him and the fur on the end of its very long tail was tickling his nose. It tickled so much it made him sneeze.

"What were you dreaming about?" the squirrel asked. "Only you were smiling the very biggest of smiles."

"If you must know, I think I have fallen in love. I met this most beautiful mouse this morning and I can't stop thinking about her."

"Ooooh! Love you say. I can tell you a thing or two about love," the squirrel replied.

"You can?" William said perking up immediately. You see William knew nothing whatsoever about love.

"Yes I can. You see I had fallen asleep on my back on the branch of an elm tree after a particularly fulfilling lunch of acorns. Then a spider dangled down from his web and landed on my face – I hate spiders you see – and I was so taken by surprise that I fell off the branch and landed right next to a very pretty squirrel who was sitting beneath the tree."

"Oh dear," said William, "were you hurt?"

"No, no, not at all thankfully, you see the branch was quite low to the ground and luckily I missed the lady squirrel by only the smallest amount – a millimetre possibly."

"That was lucky. Go on, you were going to tell me about love."

"Love, yes, that's right, I was going to tell you wasn't I. As soon as I set eyes on Peaches that was it, I couldn't leave her. Luckily for me she felt the same for old Nutkin here and we got married last spring."

"That's a lovely story," said William. "But how on earth will I know if Minka feels the same way about me? I have only met the one time and I have absolutely no idea how she feels."

"That's easy. Go and pick one of those dandelion clocks over there, hold it in your paw and start to blow. With each blow you will find a seed blows off the old flower head and all you have to say in your head is 'She Loves Me ... She Loves Me Not' and depending on what you say when the very last seed blows away you will find your answer."

"Is it really that simple?" William asked.

"Yep, it's that simple," Nutkin replied. "Well, toodleypip I have to go now or else Peaches will wonder where I have got to. She has to tend to the baby you see and I promised to bring her back some ripe acorns."

Nutkin jumped back up into the tree and scampered across the branches until he was out of sight.

William had a job to do. First he went and picked a dandelion clock and carefully carried it back to where he had been sitting. He had heard the story of telling the time by blowing on the seed head but he had never heard the one about love. He just hoped that the clock would tell him what he wanted to hear or else he was going to be very upset.

He took in a deep breath and gently blew the seed head. As the first seeds blew away he recited inside his head "She Loves Me ... She Loves Me Not" until there were only two seeds left. He stopped blowing because he was very nervous that it would end with 'She Loves Me Not'. His heart was pounding again as he took the last blow.

As the single seed drifted off in the breeze he said out loud this time "She Loves Me ..." and his heart sank because he knew when the final seed blew away it would mean 'She Loves Me Not'. He delayed blowing the last

seed for a very long time but in the end he knew it had to be done and he puffed and puffed but the seed would not budge.

I think that's my sign, William thought, and I didn't use any magic.

William was so happy that he lay back on the grass and listened to all the animals around him going about their daily life. He could hear the ribbeting of a couple of frogs in the pond, many birds singing but most of all a pigeon calling to his mate in the familiar words of 'Where's Old Sid', or at least that's what his father had told him they said.

He must have drifted off to sleep with happy thoughts because when he woke there was a chill in the air and the sun was already sinking behind the horizon. He was a little bit cross with himself for falling asleep because he had been determined to get to Trickle Wallop before nightfall. Now he had to find somewhere else to spend the night and he had run out of food.

But then he thought of his magic suitcase. He had one wish left. He didn't need to use it to see Minka again because he already knew where she lived and he had now discovered that she loved him too. That would have to wait for another day. He made the decision then and there to use his last wish to take him to his cousin's house in Trickle Wallop.

He packed away his belongings, closed the case, rubbed it three times in a circular motion and chanted the words 'Rumtirarra-grant-me-a-wish' three times and waited for the flash of blue light. It seemed to take forever and William wondered whether his last wish was going to fail, but suddenly the familiar sound of popping bubbles was followed by the blue swirling mist and he was being whisked away in some sort of tornado. How did it know where I wanted to go, William wondered because he hadn't actually wished a wish?

Round and round he went, until his head hurt and he felt slightly sick. Just when he thought he couldn't take any more it stopped and William was suddenly standing outside the prettiest little cottage with a grass roof and walls made from mud and straw. There was a little round door in the centre and one window which revealed a pale yellow flickering light inside. He hoped it meant that his cousin was at home, after all it was dark now. He peered through the window and there sitting in a comfortable chair by a little log fire was cousin Peanut. He hadn't seen him in about five years, but he recognised him straight away.

He rapped on the window gently and Peanut looked to see what the noise was. It was rare for him to get visitors, especially at night. When he saw William's face peering out from the darkness he jumped out of his chair, ran to the door and gave him the biggest mouse hug in the world.

"William, my dear cousin, what on earth are you doing here?"

"You didn't get my letter then?" William asked.

"Letter, no, what letter?"

"Ah, well, I suppose I didn't expect it to arrive because I didn't really know your address."

"Then how on earth did you find me?" Peanut asked curiously.

William proceeded to tell him all about his adventures and the three wise mice and his magic suitcase.

Peanut wasn't sure whether to believe him about all of his stories because his cousin had always been one for making up good tales, but he enjoyed listening to him anyway.

They talked and talked until they were too tired to talk any more. They had a lovely hot cup of chestnut broth with some cheese biscuits and then went off to bed. William was so happy and Peanut was delighted that his cousin had come to stay. William fell asleep dreaming of Minka and all the adventures he and Peanut were going to have. He had been really surprised to learn that Trickle Wallop was right on the coast and that in the morning Peanut had promised to take him swimming right after breakfast.

William hadn't told Peanut about Minka straight away because he had been so pleased to see him he hadn't wanted to alarm him that he might be going away again. He would keep that story for another day.

The next morning Peanut and William both had a hearty breakfast and then put on their swimming clothes. Well, actually William didn't have any, so Peanut said he could wear his spare pair which were more like a pair of stripy pyjamas. Peanut himself wore a little sailor suit and hat.

They ran down to the beach hand-in-hand and danced like children on the sand. They made sandcastles, skimmed pebbles across the water and dabbled their toes in the cold water. Every time a wave came they ran backwards screaming, trying to escape the water as it crept up the beach. William was in heaven. Why oh why hadn't he moved to the country before?

Every day they had adventures, every day they laughed, every day they were thankful to be together.

Summer turned to autumn and the leaves started to drop from the trees. Reds, golds, browns and greens made a multi-coloured carpet on Peanut's lawn. There was a bit of a chill in the air but that didn't stop William and Peanut going out into the garden and rolling around in the leaves. They made so much noise with their laughter, the nextdoor neighbour came out and decided to join in. Peanut even had a go at juggling the leaves after William's story about the circus, but the wind just kept blowing them away which made them laugh even more.

Only one thing spoilt William's happiness and that was that he still couldn't stop thinking about Minka and her beautiful brown eyes.

He was frightened if he told Peanut about her it would spoil their relationship and he would be jealous, so William kept it to himself. Then one day Peanut caught William looking a little sad sitting on his bed with a wistful look in his eyes.

"William, what's wrong? Aren't you happy? Are you feeling homesick for the city?" Peanut asked sitting down by his side.

"Oh, Peanut, I am so happy sometimes it makes me want to cry, but I do have something to tell you and I don't want you to get upset."

"Upset, why on earth would I get upset?" Peanut said putting his paw on his cousin's knee.

William took a deep breath and decided to tell him about Minka.

"You see, Peanut, there is one story I didn't tell you about my journey to get to Trickle Wallop."

"Go on," Peanut urged him, intrigued to know why he would keep anything secret from him.

"While I was in the village of Gallumpton I met the most beautiful mouse in the whole world. You know I have never really had any feelings for a girl mouse before, but somehow this mouse was different. Her name was Minka. I only spoke with her for a few minutes before she had to get on the bus, but I did find out where she lived, and that was above the Post Office with her cousin and her son. I didn't know for sure whether she felt the same way about me until a squirrel told me the secret of the dandelion clock and then I knew for sure."

"The dandelion clock, I thought that only told the time?" Peanut said a little confused.

"So did I," William continued. "However, if you blow the seed head and repeat over and over 'She Loves Me ... She Loves Me Not' until the last seed head blows away you will know whether you have found your true love."

"And yours, where did that end?" Peanut asked.

"With 'She Loves Me' and now I think it is time for me to go and find her and ask her to be my bride."

"Why the sad face William?" Peanut asked patting his knee. "This is simply wonderful news. And I don't think you should waste another minute."

"You mean you don't mind, you're not jealous?" William said in a surprised tone.

"Not in the least. In fact I am overjoyed and I am going to start to build you a house right next to mine as soon as you leave for Gallumpton."

William couldn't help the tears that trickled down his cheeks. He had never met anyone as generous and loving as Peanut and now he was prepared to help him even more. He hugged him until he had no hugs left in him.

William prepared to leave the very next morning, only this time he didn't have to walk, go by boat, or bicycle because Peanut lent him his car. It was Peanut's pride and joy, his little blue sports car, but he cared so much about William and his happiness that he was more than happy for him to borrow it to drive to Gallumpton.

Just before he left, Peanut asked him to wait a moment because he had one more thing he wanted to give him. He went inside the house and came out moments later carrying something in the palm of his hand.

"What's this Peanut?" William asked.

"It's a little gold ring that used to belong to my grandmother," he said. "I have always known it would come in useful one day and I want you to have it. I shall have no need for it I have everything I want, especially now you are here."

Once again the tears threatened to well up in his eyes, but he managed to blink them back. He put the ring into his blazer pocket, put his glasses on the end of his nose and drove off in the direction of Gallumpton.

When he arrived at the Post Office, William almost lost his nerve. Maybe he had just imagined that she felt the same way about him and that the dandelion clock was nothing but a trick. Oh how he wished he had one more wish left in his little green suitcase to make everything turn out all right.

He was about to knock on the front door when something made him step back and look up at the front window. A blackbird had caught his attention by pecking on the glass and as he looked up he saw Minka standing there her eyes wide in surprise. She did a little wave and then opened the window.

"Hello Minka," William said.

"Hello William," she said blushing ever so slightly. At least she had remembered his name which William saw as a good sign.

"Can you come down and talk?" he asked, crossing his fingers behind his back for luck.

Minka nodded, shut the window and asked him to wait for a couple of minutes while she spoke to her cousin to see if she could manage the Post Office for a little while.

It seemed to take forever before Minka appeared in the doorway. She was wearing the prettiest dress and bonnet and William still couldn't get over her enormous brown eyes. He thought she was probably a little younger than himself, but not by much which was a good thing because he really was starting to get a few wrinkles around the eyes.

"Do you think we could go for a little walk down by the river?" William asked.

"Yes, that would be lovely," Minka replied and pulled her hat a little further over her eyes to hide them from the sun and also to conceal the blushes. She wasn't used to being in the company of a male mouse on her own and for some strange reason he made her heart flutter.

They walked and talked as if they had known each other for ever and eventually reached the river. Minka had bought a picnic and they sat on a mossy spot on the bank and learned a little more about each other. By the time they had finished eating the sun was starting to hide behind the trees and the air was cooling down. It wasn't quite summer and the evenings were still cool.

William saw Minka do a little shiver and took off his jacket and placed it around her shoulders.

"That's very kind of you William, thank you."

"I want to be kind to you for the rest of my life, Minka. Do you think you could ever consider marrying me even though we have only just met? I really don't think I want to live without you in my life."

Minka really blushed this time and William saw a tear in the corner of her eye. He had a funny feeling she was going to say no and he could feel his heart sinking like a stone.

She was silent for quite a long time and every time William went to say something she put a little finger to his lips and said, "Shhhh."

William thought he was going to go mad and in the end he stood up and started pacing up and down, up and down, up and down until he had worn a path in the moss. He was just about to turn and pace for the umpteenth time when he felt a tiny paw take hold of his.

"William, I would be very proud to become your wife," Minka said. "I'm sorry it took so long to make up my mind but you see I have always taken my time over important decisions. And this is a very important decision."

William nearly jumped for joy and didn't know what to say, so instead he bent down and kissed her very gently on the cheek.

The wedding was arranged for the first day of June and Peanut insisted on making all the arrangements. He built a tiny archway at the bottom of his garden – he was very good at building things – and covered it with wild flowers that he collected from the meadows near his home. He had asked the local dormouse to marry them because he had a special licence and Minka's cousin had agreed to do all the catering for the day.

William was so nervous when the day arrived that he couldn't do up his special blue silk tie. He really was all fingers and thumbs.

"Come here," said Peanut, "let me do that for you."

He had hired a black jacket and top hat and he had polished his glasses specially for the occasion.

When Minka arrived, driven by her cousin, the sight of her took William's breath away. She was wearing the palest of blue dresses, with a daisy in her hair and a daisy chain wound all the way up her tail to the very tip. She had pretty pink lips and William thought she was the most beautiful thing he had ever seen.

After the ceremony there was dancing and eating, and then more eating, and then they all drank elderberry wine which Peanut had made specially for the occasion. It was one of the best days of William's life.

Peanut had one last surprise for William and Minka and he didn't tell them until the end of the day when all the guests had left. He told them to take his little blue car and follow the directions on the map he had left in the glovebox.

"Where are we going?" asked Minka.

"It's a surprise," said Peanut, "but I know you will both love it."

So the pair drove off with a banner on the back of Peanut's little blue car saying M ♥ W and loads of empty tin cans which clattered on the road as they drove away. Peanut waved madly with a big smile on his face. He had arranged for them to stay in a hobbit style house right in the middle

of nowhere. It belonged to his best friend who said he would be more than happy to move out for a week. He left a bottle of pink strawberry champagne, plenty of cheese and loads of other goodies to keep them going while they were on honeymoon.

While they were away, Peanut put the finishing touches to their new home. It was the prettiest little house with a straw roof and walls made from mud and straw to keep out the wind and rain. He gave them a little round front door which he made out of oak and carved their initials underneath the door knocker. As he promised, the house was right next to his own so he would never have to be without his favourite cousin again. And now he had an extra friend in Minka. Life was good.

William and Minka had a whole week to themselves and thanks to Peanut a beautiful place to stay. They walked in the countryside, had picnics by the river and in the evening William would read Minka a story from his favourite mouse book 'The Dimwood Chronicles'. How his life had changed since he left the crowded streets of London and he wondered if the little homeless mouse was still sleeping in his larger yellow suitcase. As for the little green magic case – well – William had no use for wishes any more as all his dreams had come true. It really was a very special suitcase and it had got him out of a pickle on more than one occasion.

Do you know the first thing Minka did when they got back to their new home? After letting William carry her across the threshold she said, "I am going to have a bath in my very own bathroom."

"Why?" asked William curiously.

"Because, my darling William, I have never had a bathroom to call my own," and she gave him a quick kiss and went to get her mop cap. William filled the bath with plenty of bubbles, left her a towel nearby and went downstairs while his beautiful wife made herself even more beautiful. He smiled – it was the perfect end to his wanderings.

BATH
SOAP

Printed in Great Britain
by Amazon